S0-APP-376

Darlene

DISCARD
Ryder School Library
Cobleskill, New York

Darlene

Eloise Greenfield

**Illustrated by
George Ford**

 Methuen, New York

Other books by Eloise Greenfield:

I Can Do It by Myself (with Lessie Jones Little)
Honey, I Love
Africa Dream
First Pink Light
Me and Neesie
She Come Bringing Me That Little Baby Girl

Library of Congress Cataloging in Publication Data

Greenfield, Eloise.
 Darlene.

 SUMMARY: Once she starts having fun with her
uncle and cousin, a young girl, who is confined to
a wheelchair, is no longer anxious to go home.
 [1. Physically handicapped – Fiction] I. Ford,
George Cephas. II. Title.
PZ7.G845Dar   [E]   80-15922
ISBN 0-416-30701-9

Copyright © 1980 by Eloise Greenfield
Illustrations copyright © 1980 by George Ford
No part of this publication may be reproduced, stored
in a retrieval system, or transmitted in any form or
by any means electronic, mechanical, photocopying,
recording, or otherwise without prior written permission
from the Publisher.
Manufactured in the United States of America

First Edition

Published in the United States of America by
Methuen, Inc.
733 Third Avenue
New York, N.Y. 10017

3 9014 30002 1108

For the students at
Sharpe Health School in Washington, D. C.

and for
Alesia Ann Revis

For Tchad, Shawna,
Olivia

Darlene wanted to go back home.

Uncle Eddie said,
"Your mama's coming to get you at two o'clock."

Her cousin Joanne said, "Come on, let's play."

But Darlene said, "I want to go home!"

"Wait until two o'clock," Uncle Eddie said.

So Darlene played a game with her cousin Joanne.

Then she asked Uncle Eddie, "Is it two o'clock yet?"

Uncle Eddie said, "Not yet."

So Darlene played another game

with her cousin Joanne.

Then she asked Uncle Eddie, "Is it two o'clock yet?"

Uncle Eddie said, "No, not yet."

So Darlene played one more game

with her cousin Joanne.

Then she asked Uncle Eddie, "Isn't it two o'clock yet?"

But Uncle Eddie said, "Not quite yet."

So Uncle Eddie played his guitar and Darlene sang songs
with her cousin Joanne, and then

the doorbell rang, and Mama was back.

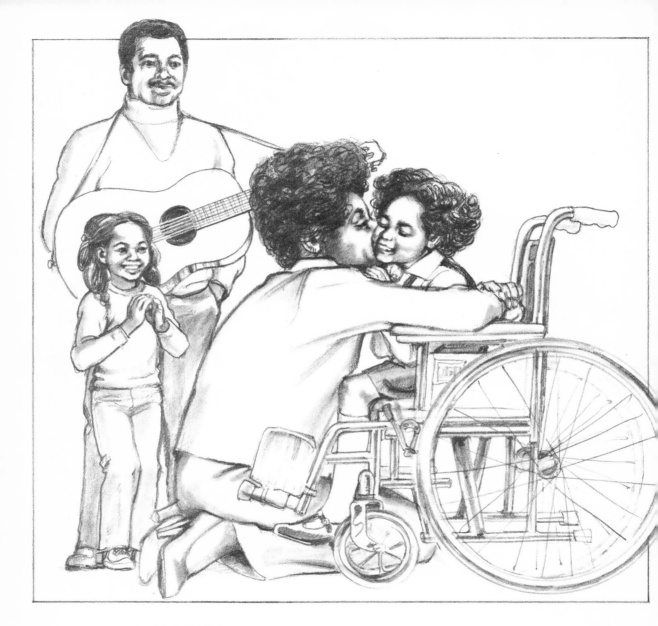

Uncle Eddie said,
    "Now, Darlene, you can go back home."

Darlene looked at her Uncle Eddie
  and she looked at her cousin Joanne and she said,

"I don't want to go home!"

Uncle Eddie said,
"Darlene, you don't know *what* you want."

But Darlene said, "Yes, I do.
      I want to change my mind when I want to."

Uncle Eddie laughed and Joanne laughed
and Mama laughed

and then they all sat down and sang songs.

And the one that sang the loudest was Darlene.

DISCARD
84-411
Ryder School Library
Cobleskill, New York

The artist thanks Ms. Shirley Johnson, Director of the
Muscular Dystrophy Association, and Dr. Oscar H. Ciner,
Professor of Health Sciences and Director of Health Services
at Long Island University, Brooklyn Center, New York.